## Taste Bud Pledge

"I promise to keep my mind open and my fork ready, to try each new food at least two times, and to share what's on my plate when someone doesn't have enough."

This story is for Chef Kyo Pang, who inspires me daily
with her food, her friendship, her wisdom, and her
indomitable spirit of generosity and love. —S.T.

For my brother, Michael, and my mom, Cathy,
who keep me creative, interested, and laughing —J.K.E.

Copyright © 2022 by Kalamata's Kitchen, LLC
Illustrations by Jo Kosmides Edwards

All rights reserved. Published in the United States by Random House Children's Books,
a division of Penguin Random House LLC, New York.

Random House and the colophon are registered trademarks of Penguin Random House LLC.
Kalamata's Kitchen® is a registered trademark of Kalamata's Kitchen, LLC.

Visit us on the Web! rhcbooks.com
Educators and librarians, for a variety of teaching tools, visit us at RHTeachersLibrarians.com

Library of Congress Cataloging-in-Publication Data is available upon request.
ISBN 978-0-593-30795-3 (trade) — ISBN 978-0-593-30796-0 (lib. bdg.)
ISBN 978-0-593-30797-7 (ebook)

MANUFACTURED IN CHINA   10 9 8 7 6 5 4 3 2 1   First Edition

# Kalamata's KITCHEN®

## Taste Buds in Harmony

Written by **Sarah Thomas**

Co-created by **Derek Wallace**   Illustrated by **Jo Kosmides Edwards**

Random House 🏠 New York

It was a beautiful day in Kalamata's kitchen.
A perfect day, in fact, to practice a dance routine
with her friends for the upcoming talent show.
   But despite everyone's best intentions, practice
was not going perfectly.

Dovie insisted that the routine needed more twirls. Knox wanted more break dancing, but he was the only one who could do the moves. Kalamata thought they should rename the group "the Dal-apeño Poppers." Kyo just wanted everyone to get along, but nobody was listening. Everyone *did* agree that Al Dente was hogging the spotlight—and that it was definitely time for a snack.

Dovie and Knox went next door for their snack, while Kyo and Kalamata dug into the beautiful Baba Nyonya kuih* that had been sent by Kyo's mummy. They were Kyo's favorite Malaysian sweets.

Kalamata let out a frustrated sigh. "Why won't anyone listen to me? My idea is MUCH more important than adding extra twirls!"

*You say it like this: "BA-ba NO-nya KWAY"

"But Dovie thinks *her* idea is more important than anyone else's!" said Kyo as she pulled apart the layers of a kuih lapis. "I don't know who is right. But I've always heard that if we don't start with good energy, it won't turn out right, either!"

"So if we can't figure out how to get along, the dance will be a disaster!" Kalamata exclaimed. "We can't let that happen. But how do we get everyone to work together?"

The girls thought hard. "Sometimes when my mummy cooks, I don't know how the different ingredients will go together," said Kyo. "But in the end, it is always so delicious. It's like she has magic in her hands!"

*Magic? In her hands?*

Kalamata had an idea. "We need to find the magic in our group! Maybe if we can find it in your mummy's food, we can get everyone to work together. Come on, Kyo, let's go!"

Grown-ups didn't know, but Kalamata's kitchen table was *also* magical. Under it, Kalamata, Al Dente, and Kyo could go anywhere. All they had to do was close their eyes, and something delicious would happen. . . .

When they opened their eyes, they were surrounded by a riot of beautiful sights, smells, and sounds from the Baba Nyonya ingredients in Kyo's family's kopitiam\*.

"Everything looks so perfect in your mummy's restaurant, Kyo! Where do we even start?"

\*You say it like this: "ko-pi-tee-um"

RICE  RICE  RICE

The sharp scents of lime leaves and tamarind
pricked their noses and drew them closer.

"It's so **ZINGY** and **ZIPPY** and **BRIGHT**!" exclaimed the Taste Buds, smacking their lips from the tangy tamarind.

"It makes me feel like I could shoot lightning from my fingers!" shouted Kalamata excitedly. "Maybe *this* is where the magic in your mummy's hands comes from!"

"But it's never just zingy-lightning-bright when she cooks," said Kyo. "It's like the *sour* helps everything else shine, too."
"Then let's find out what else we need! I think the tang made my tongue more excited for the next taste!"

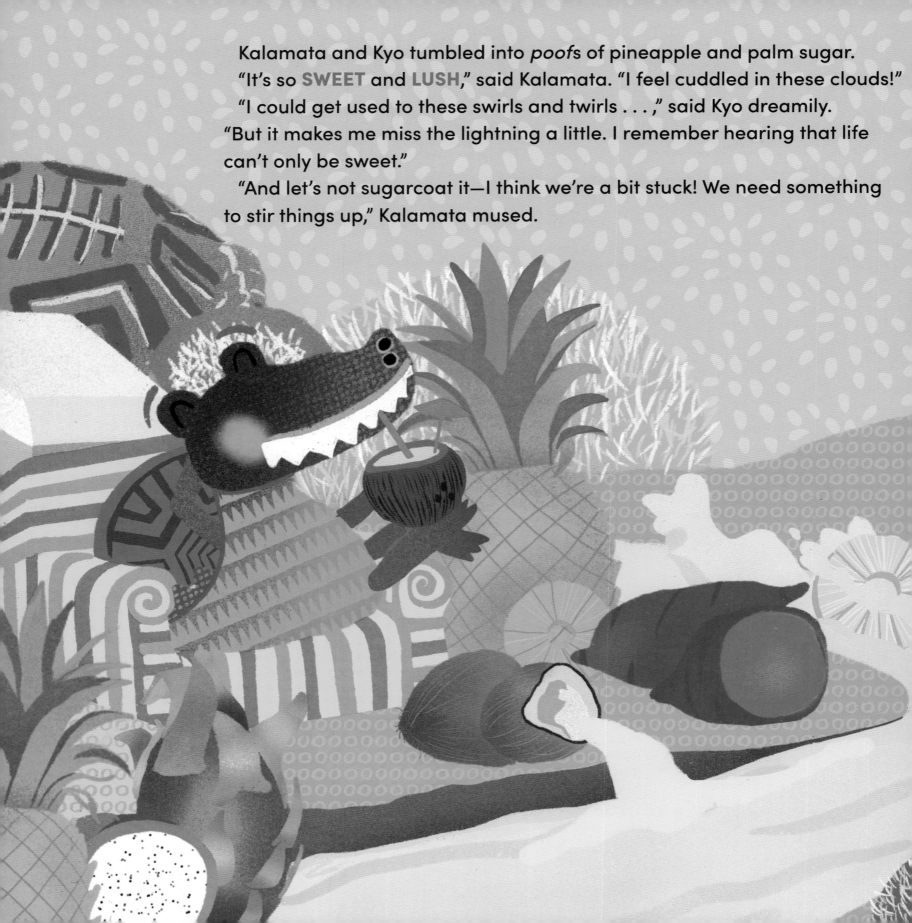

Kalamata and Kyo tumbled into *poof*s of pineapple and palm sugar.

"It's so **SWEET** and **LUSH**," said Kalamata. "I feel cuddled in these clouds!"

"I could get used to these swirls and twirls . . . ," said Kyo dreamily. "But it makes me miss the lightning a little. I remember hearing that life can't only be sweet."

"And let's not sugarcoat it—I think we're a bit stuck! We need something to stir things up," Kalamata mused.

Kyo, Kalamata, and Al jumped into a tango of chilies. The excitement was electric, and the team couldn't help but tap their toes in tempo.

"It's so TINGLY and FIERY and makes me want to learn some new moves!" said Kyo.

"That's one way to put the pepper in our steppers!" exclaimed Kalamata.

"I'm not sure how much more I can handle, though," said Kyo, panting. "If I were this excited all the time, I'd be so tired!"

"It's heating up in here, for sure. But if there's too much of this, maybe we won't be able to taste anything else. How do we keep it under control?" wondered Kalamata.

"I know what we need to cool things down!" said Kyo.
The team followed as she plunged into the salty sea.
They bobbed and whirled with the waves.
"It's so **SPRITZY** and **SAVORY** and brings it
all together!" shouted Kyo.

The
Dal-apeño
Poppers!

They breathed in the salty sea air and smacked their lips.

"Too much and it's all we'd taste, but just the right amount could *cure* us!" exclaimed Kalamata.

"Like a perfect finishing touch," declared Kyo.

Everything they needed to create something delicious was right in front of them—but how did it all fit together? The team considered their next moves.

"What if we pulled in the pineapple?"
"Ripe idea! The salt makes the sweet taste sweeter!"
"And then we warm it up with some chilies?"
"Yes! The sweet beats the heat *just* enough!"
"And to bring it all to life—maybe the tamarind?"
"Zippee! That *zing* is like we added sunshine to the sauce!"

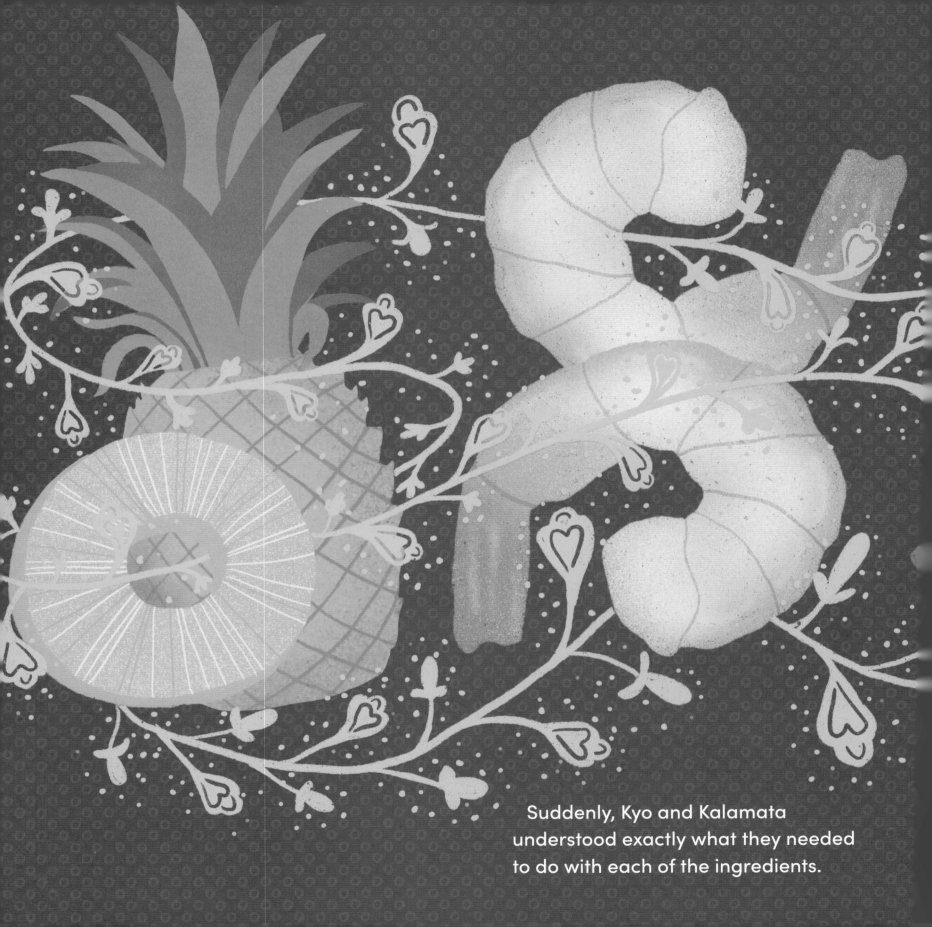

Suddenly, Kyo and Kalamata
understood exactly what they needed
to do with each of the ingredients.

"Kyo, I think we found the magic in your mummy's hands. She knows that every ingredient is special, but they're all better when they work together!

"And you know what?" continued Kalamata. "Dovie was right—
our dance *could* use more twirls! And we can all break-dance,
too, if Knox just teaches us his moves! If we all work together, this
will be the fan-tastiest dance the world has ever seen!"

In Kalamata's kitchen, the snack break was over. Dovie and Knox arrived back just as the Taste Buds reemerged from under the table. The smell of udang curry nanas filled the air.

"We're so happy you're back!" said Kalamata. "We think we've found the missing magic in our team."

"Missing magic?" asked Dovie.

"What do you mean?" asked Knox.

"She means we *all* have something to bring to the table!" said Kyo.

"That's right!" said Kalamata, smiling. "Each of us has something that will make the whole team shine! If we put all our ideas—and our moves!—together, we'll win together, too."

"Now, *that's* a yummy idea!" shouted Knox and Dovie. The team high-fived and got to work.

# THE DAL-APEÑO POPPERS

And with swirls, twirls, and a brand-new move called the pepper grinder, the Dal-apeño Poppers stole the show.

# Udang Curry Nanas (Pineapple Prawn Curry)

By Chef Kyo Pang

- 20 long red Holland chilies, stems removed
- ⅓ cup roasted belachan powder (shrimp paste)
- 10 cloves garlic
- 16 small shallots, roughly chopped (about 2 cups)
- 4 stalks fresh lemongrass, bottom parts only, with tough outer leaves removed (or ⅓ cup lemongrass powder)
- 2-inch piece galangal (about 2 oz.), peeled and roughly chopped
- 2 tbsp. turmeric powder
- 2 tbsp. curry powder

- 4 candlenuts (optional)
- 3½ tsp. sea salt
- ¾ cup vegetable oil
- 1¾ cup coconut milk
- 1⅔ cup water
- 1 cup fresh pineapple cubes
- 1½ tbsp. tamarind paste, melted and strained with ½ cup boiled water (ask an adult to boil the water in a kettle)
- ¼ cup palm sugar
- 12–16 tiger prawns, washed, shell split along back, and deveined
- 4–6 kaffir lime leaves, thinly sliced

Put red chilies, roasted belachan powder, garlic, shallots, lemongrass, galangal, turmeric powder, curry powder, candlenuts if using, and salt into a blender. Blend, adding small amounts of water to ease the process.

Heat oil in a pan over medium heat. Sauté blended paste until it is fragrant and dark orange.

Add coconut milk and water, and stir until incorporated.

Gently add pineapple cubes, and simmer for about 6 minutes.

Turn heat to low. Add tamarind paste and palm sugar, stirring so sugar is fully dissolved.

Turn heat to medium. Add prawns and half the kaffir lime leaves. Mix well. Prawns will be fully cooked when they are bright pink-orange, about 5–10 minutes.

Remove from heat. Add remaining kaffir lime leaves as garnish.

Serve with coconut rice.

# One Last Bite!

The inspiration for this story came from my friend Chef Kyo Pang. Kyo's family and her Baba Nyonya Malaysian heritage have influenced her understanding of harmony, balance, and love through food and in life, and it is conveyed with such joy in every dish she makes. Here are just a few of the ideas she shared with me about the Baba Nyonya philosophy on food.

**Good Energy:** "Philosophy, religion, and food are all connected for Baba Nyonya families. We believe beginning a task with good energy means it will be accomplished with good energy. For that reason, we try not to make negative comments while someone is making kuih—you don't want the negativity to affect the flavor. We also believe the hands are connected to the soul, and cooking with your hands is an extension of your heart. The food you make with love and positivity puts that good energy into the people who eat it."

**Harmony:** "I think food can really send a message of love to people, and we believe also in the concept of zen. Zen and love together create harmony. Baba Nyonya people believe in creating harmony with one another, and that is directly reflected in our food. Each ingredient has its own characteristics and character, and each character is unique, but they work perfectly with one another if you have taken the time to understand them well. People also have their own unique ways of doing things, but we can all learn to fit together if we take the time to understand each other."

**Circles and Continuity:** "Circles and spheres are very important in our culture. We like things to be round because circles connect people. They represent good things coming around and a return to your origins. It helps you realize that everything is connected and continuous. A return to my origins has helped me realize who I really am, and I try to express what I've learned from my culture in my food so other people can experience it, too."

# An Introduction to Nyonya Kuih

Kuih, sometimes also called kue or kueh, are traditional sweet or savory snacks that are found all over Malaysia, Indonesia, and Singapore. Kuih are considered a specialty of the Baba Nyonya people. Made with ingredients such as rice flour, mung beans, coconut milk, fragrant pandan, and blue butterfly pea blossoms, there's a tender, squishy, colorful, salty, or sweet kuih for everyone to love! Here are just a few of the many varieties of Nyonya kuih found in Malaysia.

KUIH BAKAR

ANG KU KUIH

KUIH BONGKONG

KUIH DADAR

KUIH KOSUI

KUIH TALAM

KUIH LAPIS

PULUT TAI TAI

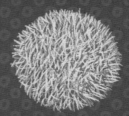

KUIH ONDEH ONDEH

KUIH LAPIS LEGIT